WANDERING TOWARD A PREARRANGED DESTINY

Bilingual Expeditions from the Heart

By

Richard Alberto Morillo Guevara-Fabra'

Andrea T. Goldreyer

Editor

James A. Morillo

Co-editor

Cover Illustration By

"AL GUINZAGUO" 2019 On a Leash Carlo Salomoni Pittore/Illustratore/Scultore/Progettista Carlosalomoni@gmail.com *Mobile +39 3393947367 Ferrara, Italia.*

Cover Design by Elieshka Kocendova; elieshkadesign.com

PUBLISHED by SOUTHERN MOUNTAINS PUBLISHING Ltd Merrick, New York. USA

Library of Congress Control Number

201990020242

ISBN 978-0-9863863-5-0

United States of America Copyright 2019

DEDICATION

This book of Poetry is dedicated to the hundreds of poets who had a personal, diverse and powerful influence not only in my life but also writing such as: Langston Hughes, Pablo Neruda, Ervin Cerny, Gwendolyn Brooks, Eugenio Montale, Robert Frost, Walt Whitman, Amy Lowell, Nelly Sachs, Cesar Vallejo, Salvatore Quasimodo, Anne Sexton, Henri Michaux, Louis Aragon, Vaclav Havel, T. S. Eliot, Anna Akhmatova, Karila Galvez, Alfonsina Storni, Wallace Stevens, Ruben Dario, Medardo Angel Silva, Silvia Plath, Elsie Lasker-Schuler, Elinor Wylie , Jose Carrera Andrade, Vicente Huidobro and Amy Levy among hundred others whose breathtaking talent wealth of made an early and eager participant in search of new images that would help me afford escape the complex nature of my childhood and beyond.

This book is also dedicated to my Professors, Dr. Antonio Sacoto Salamea at C.C.N.Y. and 2010 Nobel Prize winner in Literature Mario Vargas Llosa at Columbia University who inspired and challenged me academically while encouraging me to never stop working on my craft.

WANDERING TOWARD A PREARRANGED DESTINY

Bilingual Expeditions from the Heart

WANDERING TOWARD A PREARRANGED DESTINY
Bilingual Expeditions from the Heart

Table of Contents

TELL ME YOUR STORY

*I am the child of firestorms, of yester time with faith in falling stars.
I've survived the mystery of an experimental childhood and a
weekend of intentional fading light under the doomed
stranded domain in the heavens.*

*I was monitored under the watchful eye of forest dwellers in outer
space plowing in oceans of meteors. An influx of magical
spirits attempted to kidnap my voracious imagination
that since has not been deleted.*

*I've journeyed through undiscovered fields on ancient lands hauling
beliefs of modern witchcraft, vehicles of misinformation and
folklore; a berth and place of superstition where auctions of
souls take place, the loser going with the self-righteous.*

*I've explored the transformed ready to recite prayers for adults that
target the weak and exploited for some remote reunion
at the margins of a distant nebulous horizon
fraught with fraudulent promises.*

*I've come of age now. I have opened my eyes to the deceptions that
have been rendered from the emerging mutterings of those
in various uniforms with epaulets and vain crosses.*

*I am arriving to dreams and unforeseen realities arisen out of the ashes
of darkened covered books and misrepresented Atlases of non-existed
worlds roaring to spill their own distorted lies fueled by their
own consumptive dogmas.*

*I'm awake. I see the gap between those that can and will, and those
that can't and won't. In front of me, I see the collapse of the spirit
of the helpless targeted by war and famine in the name
of shared security and progress.*

What will become of our lives, and what will happen to our souls?

June 01, 1971 – April 01, 1982

AT THE OUTSET OF A JOURNEY

As I pass the wooden corridors filled with ghostly stillness, a shapeless mass of burning… fading, plagued silence awaits me.

A long and thick forest of soundless notes accost me for what seems to be long hours of purgatory before I awaken to wonders.

I endlessly walk streets that already have my name, as I weave light post after light post, mapping a nimble journey at the edge of avid gardens.

Sullen winds wander, circling past the ashen landscape filled with air currents that bring immolated dreams as compost for a whispering Earth.

I navigate on rails ignited by the brush fires in the night sky, breathing distances created from the outset of our primal mutterings.

Miles and miles away from completing my destiny, a stirring dusk is piercing the roots of my brawling fathomless future in collision with the Earth.

Invisible ghosts are still approaching my imminent unfolding / barricaded bay where I am swashbuckling my own roaring shadow.

September 16, 2013

A NEW LIGHT IS COMING TO OUR SHORE

The evergreen rustling from the cold and lonely wind is peering behind the planted weeping willow garden where the longing heart's despair preys on the diminishing unadorned light.

The dangling moss belonging to thunderbolts of life with untraceable footprints is attempting to replicate this land's splendor by coating it in laden rain… clear, unwrapped, purifying god's river pale water.

Listen to the truth in my eyes and the voice of my longing heart, as well as rain that I hold in my hands for you to drink from. Don't be afraid. It's clear naked water for your body to navigate in and cleanse its ailing soul.

A new light is imminent to help you measure distances between solemn births and the emergence of darken promises buried in a graveyard of wonderment and harsh imagery. Gauge the buoyant light by its radiance traveling in our direction.

Grimaces dispossessed from my face are being corralled to chime-in the time before the shoreline's water edge, as the light of dawn is plucked from the shadow's form pouring before the landscape and its hierarchical sapling.

The howling geography is gaining ground on our own quarry, before the twilight overcomes its tender light to mend our drenching autumns soul's shore. The abstract light is awakening in our eyes so we can see the future.

Let's chant and meditate to break the chains of uncertainty, before our next frail voyage past sunless walls, wrought iron windows and approaching strain. There's always hope and everlasting solace past toothless shadows.

Agile graceful light will guide us to new shores.

All our descendants were birds!

April 19, 1982

EXILED TRANSLATIONS

Buoyed by the thunder, my voice sings. It defies exiled translations while rhyming and prestidigitating, guarding my night songs.

I row in oceans of shadows sweeping the riverbanks of my heart and brain, just as myth references my history to cast its spell in other tongues.

Mistranslations live in the barren auditory lands where I guard the night inside where the sun rests, between the teeth of my temples.

Oxen landscapes in form of twigs of a bird's nest are hanging outside a blind secret letter garden devouring stolen word.

Exiled translations are reading the palm lines of the earth meandering while traversing throughout our self-contained flesh.

Language renditions full of life and critical explorations, dichotomies, analogies and images of faraway messages outside of the realm of other same worlds are tied by and with blood!

Exiled translations in transition...

August 12, 2015

THE FUTURE

The old forlorn voices of my past are raining from the sky chaperoned by
noisy scythes, the moon's rustic skin and its disintegrating skeleton.

Everything is dripping so densely and swiftly, they are wrapping the earth's
crust and all its sunflowers. They are quilting new landscapes and sending
messages to the shores of my eyes creating ephemeral new visions.

Fugitive benign voices are being patrolled by pink felines lurking in the night.
They are summoned by the new panorama dragged by rusted anchors
flanked by a distant twilight in an amber horizon.

The door to the crevices of the earth are patulous so all diced stones and
shadows can descend and go into hiding.

The multiplicity of stillness and silence is marauding the planet. Singed
grasses are unfurling themselves as eloquent premonitions.
The earth and its wounded black eyes are being cauterized.

Let's prepare for echoes of lightning that force us to fly our arms
and souls at half-staff.

Hold hands, flee this labyrinth... let's drink a spoonful of river water
and return to our mutated remote origins.

A storm is asunder!

May 30, 1973 – July 29, 2014

A PROLOGUE TO OUR EXISTENCE

We ambulate with hidden dreams, before we reveal what might be?
We could have been awake to respond by breathing before
weeping as a requisite to riding onto and beyond the
unfurling dawn and plodding disheveled sunset.

A tapestry of deeds does not precede us.
Nor a dormant birth, nor a scarlet burial in a glass chasm!

December 16, 1988

I WAS BORN

*I was born on the riverside of a lonely river as a product of a
grinding squirming wounded dream.*

*I was born as an asteroid shaped mineral that fell from another
universe's orbit only to be dragged by the lattice of a cosmic
river's current in the open sky.*

*I fell inside my mother's veins and hid in the passageways of her
aorta until a long-forgotten voice crawled from her bosom,
traveled through the synopsis in my brain and awakened
me from this singular dream.*

*The spirit of my ancestors is rising, streaking in my gasping purview.
I guess the primitive evolution must continue. I am just a gaping
organic riddle in this perpetual insurrection.*

*now the setting sun has come back, accompanied by a drifting dust.
the sweet barefoot voice of my mother pulls me once again to her
atrial geography to hold hands until the end of time.*

*the catacombs and the psalms in this cosmos' sea await us all,
but before we depart let's abduct an extra morning and
another chimera.*

Let's go on!

February 01, 1974

I AM AT THE CONFLUENCE

*I am at the confluence of ambling transmuted magic shadows
and an invented garden that instead of hanging lilies, irises
and roses, they have dangling letters on its paper branches.*

*The ripples of currents row its bouquet toward me, to intoxicate
my senses long enough so I can pluck these letters and mold
them into this dispatch.*

*Abandoned ripples of perfume bask during sunlight just before
accusatory darkness stumbles and scatters my words
in every direction.*

*I am at the junction where the missing years are lost in beseeching
conversations that are masquerading as a philosophical
conjunction with the Earth's self.*

*The association and struggle that threatens the craving for love
meet the scheme that the chambers of our heart need for
at least some fragmentary reality.*

*Our solitary structures are abdicating to rudderless winds that
will mock our wisdom for passion by appealing to drunken
gods that have never hesitated to throw us into an
endless conflagration which burns angels at the
crossroads of our grammar.*

October 01, 2015

THE BIRTH OF A BREATH

*I transmit the inescapable joy, the fierce thirst to glow as
a diamond and to rejoice.*

*I exult as the sun is fluttering, as I capture the vastness of
the infinite in conjunction with my singing and breathing
in of my own presence.*

*Clumsily but determinately I shield my scars from the
rays of rivers of centuries stirring the prophetic
songs, cries, the blood flow of rivers and fabled
shadows riding on the currents of oxygen.*

*My voice jumps over the tranquil villages with slender
solitary shadows as my dreams drive away the
birdsongs that are waking up my smile in the
distant forests in tune with my breath.*

*My breath is being plundered behind a curtain of
make believe, even as I celebrate life's launching
of a relationship with magical intermezzo
footprints among the living.*

*Am I being blasphemous for not
bartering with the gods?*

February 21, 2014

WE USE TO SOAR TOGETHER

I descend into the bottled abysses where the unprecedented narrative
of our love lies in ruins, product of the edgeless years' swells of
missed rituals, mistrusts and misled words.

Our yearning use to soar together before our love's dreams were raked
before been fully pollinated by faux bees sitting on fallen
branches ready to be set on fire.

The glowing candle lights unfastened from broken down flames are
running away from the last wicker leftover from a generation
of unfolding ardent evenings...

The spirits of the creek have impaled the fallen petals for doing illicit
dances in the presence of diminished horizons that now soar
towards forests of unchained syllables that no
longer spell H-O-M-E.

Our wireless connections are down along with the rose
petals that use to adorn your hair under unscented
weather during tribes of disappearing springs.

Are we permanently grounded? Is there hope by the
distant river?

My concealed tears are drying in the sunlight
Where tranquil halcyon shadows still dream!

September 27, 2006

WHISPERS

Frozen silence is crawling in sotto voce. Vibrations are being plucked
from water streams bridging chained articulations shackled
in captivity and felt spoken mantras.

Clinging to tones riding on grasses, armies of notes in silt, sand and clay
are confined to open-air muted stalls... looking forward to hints
of murmured anonymous springs.

Remnants of visions in distant ages are fading, peering through traces of
myths and dreams smoldering in our portals _wandering towards
prearranged destinies.

December 12, 2017

THE SUN IS TALL

Contiguous to the rivers of the sky, there are landscapes
seedlings being nurtured by the angels, and your gaze.

The sunlight's stellar height matches my heart's orbit
as it speaks during the same aphelion séance as
a final gesture of healing to all light that
populates this universe.

Restless lost secret voices are emanating from the
sun, subduing the thread of silence that is
transmitted via the sun ray's
mythological height.

The sun's affect is shimmering as a youthful companion
to this earth as it crawls over its sprawling forbidden
shadow lands.

Mislaid voices are now residing in forests of wilderness
laying open archived wounds sundried by the
ironworks of the sun hiking on
glass meadows.

August 21, 1988 - May 31, 2014

TRANSITION

My testament 's pages quiver as falling sycamore
leaves uncertain of their destiny and meaning
wrap around the veneer that intersect in the
dimming lines and my trembling wincing hand.

An earthquake is born. the dimming light hushes as it
converges with the thinning air. it is time for the
lonely shadows to hold hands as two nudes
discovering the spilling night.

I guess the moon tides will have the final say and translate
the words that play with my heart. does it really matter?
as time rocks, I'll be my ancestor's neighbor soon.
I am wounded and I snarl as I attempt to climb
out of this riptide.

Is this a designated diminished bad dream?
what nerve and irreverence.
but I am not fraying...

May 31, 1972 – November 28, 2015

RESCUED

*Behind a scarlet curtain, our love plunges in immersed
still silence in the life of dormant stones.*

*Then, it takes a stroll at night where a myriad of nude
eternities clouds its dissolving memory.*

*It's a place where our memory is turned to water so as
to be easily encapsulated inside a drop of rain.*

*Our love is a single tear dropping, vanishing in the middle
of unlit thunder just to break the silence.*

*Our love vibrates, concealing itself in hidden sleeping
life-forms intent on remaining pawned to solitude,
just to be rescued in between the shadows of a
quiet voice only heard by stones.*

April 02, 2015

ON TURNING THIRTY

*Blatant flooding Is being created to drown my freedom behind
the stone walls of shrouded flowers and cedar coffins holding
the shades and remnants of planetary secretions
creating a wasteland...*

*I drink the essence of summers long gone, desired springs and
autumns hidden and disguised as a whisper of rain. I dream
beholden to compelling passions yet to live in the
heart of an unambiguous thirsty soul.*

*Dancing with pride outside my window, I'm past the fires tolling
shattered and agreeable wonders living with foolishness;
the elixir of a young clamoring heart envisioning
victory and pain. Mercy!*

Bring it on.

May 31, 1982

DESIRE OF AN UNKNOWN MIRAGE

Grant me a kiss through framed wrought iron. Unclothe my desire
as I attempt to lengthen the night long enough to dislodge
your heart away from your smoldering dwelling.

Let me tour the contour of your figure as i journey to and fro gardens
for broken hearts along rivers from where i swallow your
nectar directly from the caldera.

Let me cradle your wings slathered with splendor, a refuge for my
soul whistling a solitary tune to sobbing moons on
our faithful journey.

Your unpainted reflection sleepwalks in front of a blind goldfinch
landing on an expatriated soil where unknown mirages
quarrel with docile muted snow-capped
cloaked messages.

The haggard seas' starlight glistening rays form an oasis of silver,
blue and the color of lavender lace as they flutter in the waves
embossed with my polychromatic heart.

Elms are tossed and drenched by the night shade that blooms in
my watering weeping eyes as they survey cross etched gushing
streams in bloom towards my desired mirage.

I am En-Route on the next train to huddle together so you can
mend the broken windowpane in my heart before
winter brushes with my crumbling bones.

Are you still there?

April 04, 2006

SURVIVING AN UPHEAVAL

*I am riddled with dismay about my un-sustaining embers, perplexed
at their sight as they fade into the blank graves streaming
away to inoculated shores for recreation.*

*I am treading as I am beckoned by the undressed confident stars
and the late moonlight reaping the sorcerer's dreams
found under clay tablets used as my pillows.*

*From the upper reaches of the universe, I find myself where the
blood of the night flows upward, as the blood to our
ventricles as a badge before moonlight*

*Canyon robes envelop the muted hidden light that shudders
behind the wretched and wounded veil by time
comingling with the briefly resurrected
shadows from the earth.*

*Out of sarcophagi, trapped ashes are flying towards urns sprinkled
with hallowed water. they are gazing at echoes of hushed
dreams and its darkened textured beams of silent
eclipses clasping unto the aroused shadows.*

*The displacement of our soul's and the earth's crust is co-mingling
as an integral manifesto crossing the seas in chase of clusters of
interrupted shadows before the upcoming enlisted cataclysm.*

*I am reckoning with and exploring for truth in the still resonant
debris floating out to the seas through the remaining time
window rendered to sleep in mid-spring.*

*Let's not weep, for we have been survivors and had our time in
the sunny fields where we have left traces of our warrior
blood in the capillaries and tissues of this universe's DNA.*

May 30, 1982 – May 31, 2012

I AM ALMOST INVISIBLE

*I was born amidst alpine sagebrush fenced in by a
blind and muted invisible history.*

*Everything about me is invisible except my burning
roots above the Earth.*

*Invisible is my shadow, except for a little sliver whose
visibility is still disarranged.*

*I don't want to get lost in sand clouds. I don't want
to be erased by unshared winds from this Earth.*

*I am nothing more than a forgotten sand particle
which has no waters to befriend.*

Unclaimed falling leaves cover my body.

I am almost invisible...

October 04, 2014

ON THE ROAD MY DUST STILL LOOKS FOR YOU

*I am avoiding walking and swimming in seas because in them, you can't
recognize nor notice my gaze, not even my footprints, nor
my dust can be seen.*

*The waves dance and they cover the bleak panorama of my ardor and desire.
The discreet silence of the sea improbably opens the windows for birds
to come in, but not here in the sea.*

*The continuous dissolution of our destiny continues. Here, the water
dissipates and removes all evidence.*

*Profoundly dense hidden replete images still live in my heart, so that I can
take them with me to look forward to seeing you past this lifetime.*

My final dust is immutable and with no redemption.

April 01, 1992

EVIDENCE

*Signposts reveal your past volcanic footprints resting on my soul.
Your aroma travels through the fibers of time, defining your
transcendence on my heart.*

*Your love was a revolutionary black and white manifesto,
reaffirmed by the loving tattoo over your heart.*

*The benevolent relevant Indications were displayed through leaks
from your eyes with the lifespan of a rose.*

*In one defining moment, the imbrued reality was conjugating at
shores of chaos and uncertain quivering waves as
tender references.
The evidence filters through from within a black and white photograph
that once we were together.*

*The debris of our disappointment parades before the remains of
undeveloped film that references our once flowering love.*

My love for you still nourishes my soul.

I still love you.

November 26, 1997 - November 26, 2014

LINE BY LINE

*Personal vein of passion and love is running through my poetry, line by line
and every strophe, sand to glass... grain by grain. Hand hewn wood
carvings of birds as well.*

*As in every seam and layer of my life, it can't be bottled because it can't be
communicated through and from serpent to porcelain dragon.*

*Arranged as deposits in a vein, bits of clay and flesh are present to
be molded, with words in the seams of the larynx of my soul.*

*I tamed my metaphors, from unfinished unembroidered memories remains
to hovering ciliatic murmurings, rhythmic waves waiting to rest. They are
shuddering truths clinging to life; measured dreams with visas ready
to travel and leap from cloud shadows of moons.*

*The light is never dim, but full of sunshine when the words play, exhort
and even bark their destined arrows thrust upon at your
wrecking baroque soul.*

*Terracotta letters are being thrown into the kiln, before walking
away as effigies transformed into Qing Dynasty Porcelain so
alive, it's making birdcalls and filling lines in this poem.*

*Holding the words in this Poem to our heart, let's close our eyes
and take a flight beyond millions of lights amidst the Milky Way
where you reside as a galactic Meteor, Comet and sacred star.*

*Ions are dancing with your and my soul along with other
solar remnants!*

May 31, 2001

BUDDING HEART

*I smell the silence howling above the unknown graves
filled with delicate pondering daffodils in cherry
gardens flowering amid the pebbles cohabiting
inside misplaced villages still whispering*

*Unplowed mountains are hiding in the broken garret of
the landscape in between the morning light and the
blowing afternoon peeling the hours away.*

*The blonde hair of the hours is editing whittled days
being twisted by waters travelling from the
budding heart of the vanishing valleys
scattering twinkling destinies.*

*Premonitions of heaping sleepless shores inhabited by
with and nameless angels are meeting to fly over
scorched memories left over barren fields
that are touching our blossoming
hearts drinking the thicket.*

*The lonely hours are whistling across the poplars and
scarce willows as cargo for our fledgling aged
freckled rivers that are driving through the
geologic parabolic bowels of the night.*

*Nascent naked prophets are pregnant with blood
vessels carrying our hopes in a basket. They are
woven with dreams from our budding hearts
been pulled toward the endless breasts
of the sun!*

November 28, 2008 – May 31, 2012

IN ALCOVES OF SILENCE

*A lukewarm murmur welcomes me accompanied by a
bouquet of caresses, which until today had remained
bottled in alcoves of silence, walled by rivers woven
and quilted in silver by the eventful history and
its rugged Orography.*

*Between fragments of forgotten petals, the inseparable
hearts and I walk pass the omitted furrows where the
passions of love spills in desired, designed and
painted abstract glaciers dancing over borders
that melt on the lines of my youth.*

*Love and loneliness are mythos, symbol of lies, desires
and myths. Yet, that's where I washed my face with
the black of the night, before removing my name
and image from the obituary notice.*

*I would love to inherit the earth before they cry
for my absence.*

December 31, 2012

THE VOICE INSIDE THE RAINDROPS

*Rushing along with just a touch of minced sarcasm, the sound
intermittently breathes water on our flesh to
make us digest mud and grime.*

*The echoes of the clatter collide with the asphalt, as a voice that
hurtles itself unto the unknowable, as swollen glands
tormenting and crashing our inner land territory.*

*In the corridors of the Earth, they manifest their power through
faded unbearable burning stones, by putting out their
fire - rigging one with the other ready to sail.*

*Gusting winds are wailing across the grasses torturing it along with
freshwater. The raindrops are caressing the roses before
returning to the earth to embrace and endure.*

*The sky's language comes in the shape of rainwater wrapped in
its skin molecules are crawling... wandering over the surface of
this land before seducing it drop by drop.*

*I can hear your voice palpitating, while grasping the process of
baptizing all the flowers without preaching to the origins
of the life of un-anchored glaciers.*

March 30, 2007

I TOO LISTEN TO THE THUNDER

*Portraits of you hunting for the battered rain once held captive
haunts my mind before the oncoming rushing tempest, a
catalyst for onrushing luscious sacramental memories.*

*I hide inside the raindrops to listen to the shifting rumble, in
search of sweet asylum in streams and passages
between the fault lines in the heavens.*

*The booming sound of thunderbolts is devouring the wretched
chains holding autumn and the evanescent content
of yours and mine dimming voice.*

*Let the journey of my love fable and storm begin accompanied
by thunder of mist, flame and passion engulf you. Let the
bellow of lighting escort us to intentional desires.*

*Let the innocence of my wandering passion move you, as the
concealed light moans in fading shadows. Let's
rumble... and create some guiltless thunder.*

Teach me how to fly.

April 01, 2007

MY VOICE AND VISION IN UNKNOWN LANDS

Voices and visions from my charred fragmented journey walk through orchards of broken spirits and loose marrow as I chronicle the frontlines of our conscience's awakening.

The signs of catastrophic rustic fog appear before me, the mapping of my existence and its hunger suffers in this unknown land.

As I uncover the transmuted landscape covered by my contaminated foreign blood, I unpack my profound silence that cries under surveillance.

As I occupy your land under control and supervision, my voice becomes muted like hollow bark, as the sands of time fill my larynx

Under scrutiny my voice and vision become brittle it collapses under the weight of my own plasma because it comes from other un-plowed lands bursting with famine and in ruins.

Although from the same planet, my voice and vision are impaled by everyone's neglect and disdain. Can my voice and remains start a bonfire in this foreign land?

Since I am invisible, Do I even need a green card to be buried? Maybe I am just a dream floating down a nameless river traversing more countries than the Danube.

May 01, 2015

LIBERATING INSIGHTS

We are moving toward open impoverished visions where swinging
pendulums have been orchestrated by past beleaguered hand-
held rivers fumbling with memories of enduring thorns
thrashing in our veins.

We've come to walk along the aquiline features of my dream's face
with a drunken stupor shadow boxing away from the
spirit's reality that eats raw memories while
praying to Earth's dust.

There is no time for permanent summaries yet, as I still have not
discovered, nor deciphered the way to the end of our
memoirs living under the moss... covered
by rapturous time.

The dusk is still a faraway empty trench where it plays and conjugates
along with the hidden sleeping fingerprints of an endless wintertime.
Solitary dances never end in the fraudulent strophes forged and
written on snow, for they are scribbled just to provide
momentary liberated insights.

We've come troubled with suggested intensity, liberated
and un-wired from our inner landscape.

April 02, 2000

I SAW MY SHADOW CRYING

*The bugles proclaim on this Earth and ask where has your
life been hiding?*

*Since my childhood I knew you playing with one of the only
two toys you had.*

*You were always very quiet, with intelligent inquisitive eyes.
Your deep-set eyes were always lucid, curious... as though
wanting to discover the world in a glance.*

*Sometimes I saw you crying inside at what you could not decipher.
Not out of frustration, but at the tantalizing new discoveries
that filled you with trepidation and excitement.*

Where are you now?

May 31, 1970

MY VOICE

My voice is unraveling. My breath is turning to vapor breaking certain provisions of history with it. It is dematerializing, and in the process weaving silence in shapes that blend in with white glaciers.

My voice melts and dances away toward abstract rivers with profane primitive names that lie beyond clouded enclosures. They descend through undisclosed clenched dreams whirling around unvisited ebony quarries that populate my imagination.

My utterances whisper their liquid tones to burgeoning agile springs, as well as to my ears and blinded eyes which went into darkness, a result of a sharpened water branch kidnapped out of a serene naked lake.

Bubbling spoonfuls of traces of sound vibrate as they go through a white doorway retreating.... emulating the tides of my voice's fate.

They are lurking and clutching onto the sweet water which with its waves will take us for a stroll over a sandy shore on the other side of the tranquil lake.

I think I'll go searching for the remnants of my voice before it completely dissipates and no longer is able to intone and murmur:
I love you.

April 01, 2015

FRAMED BY THE EVENING

*Framed by the evening I watch the parade as I talk to
trembling crustaceans whose worn distances create
sounds heard only inside my ancient soul.*

I chew the smoke of primeval time hiding in shadows.

*I am having an intimate affair with the evening while I
navigate through the map with my finger in the
framed firmament.*

*Only overgrown dandelion fences prevent my conscience
from speaking on behalf of the sometime- dislocated
night that hides forsaken souls in its foliage.*

*Everything is happening suddenly inside my head, in the
shredded residue of my collared spirit traveling in this
barren wasted landscape.*

*I gnaw the burn of primal relentless time secreted in the
midst of the kingdom of shadows.*

*Should I shake it off, wake up, or saddle and gallop away
behind the night.*

September 27, 1994 – October 11, 1996 – May 15, 2017

THE PLIGHT

Cluttered verses are fluent passengers sledding past buried vanquished overthrown dreams, long discarded by an exiled unforeseen destiny.

Strophes are abandoning their quarries out of irreverence for their fate as they bleed out of the rock to have a dialogue with the mighty oaks as well as whispers of wooden birch porches.

Fragmented sufferings are being disoriented and left vulnerable with no voice-box and interlocking fermented ideas.

Closed lips are hiding our anguish behind agitated migrant exiled homes co-habiting in peasant lands. we are spared loathsome steps only as the congregation rises next to a gathering of leaves in a hangmen's courtyard dust.

I am living next to tree branches taking a nap, as they are holding hands with the teaming perching vines careening home with early winter weather roaring towards nameless brooks.

Now I spend some time in the forest, on the other side of the earth carving out a jar of community clay, as epistles of midnight are being liberated so they can flock towards valleys where we will chew the distant horizon and the dark nights.

Let's answer to the fringes of Nordic mornings bickering silently, while they walk on oxidized ice that looks like coins in twilight playing on top of roaring waters.

Words on a manuscript are footsteps, mutterings and chanting lyrics of hope and mourning, before having a dialogue with oaks and birches about peace.

I find myself in a state of somnambulism alongside and beyond the earth's windowsills. The plight of man has pioneering stark visions and sounds of deferred hymns of hope.

I hope an avalanche of graces will soon be bestowed upon us.

February 21, 2014

STONE LOVE

I've seen your acoustically crafted voice branded on my soul.

*Amid the gentle hills, I see tired stones curled up as though
hiding from some drunken river or stumbling moon nearby.*

*I see fistfuls of the earth's filament of this universe hiding
the history of man and our past in its patina.*

I feel ancient dreams wrapped in volcanic eruptions fleeing from my destiny.

*At the edge of my sedimentary shore, the heart retreats, and in
atonement for the rain turns itself to stone!*

September 27, 1988

BEYOND BROKEN PROMISES

Assurances were given during our first limp footsteps on this planet camouflaged as our dwelling; that everything made of mud would dry and that eventually resolve itself and turn to dust.

As always, not everything you hear is true. In fact, even before the umbilical threads that tied us to our mother were broken, we found our bodies had been plundered by an onslaught of blunt vagaries, as well as docile vicissitudes.

The compilation of encounters with other humans, known and strange, defied our spontaneous evolution ravaged by early promises that oscillated between endemic fireworks of alienation trust and familiarity.

The despair conceived a crisis that attempted to explore our own myth about ourselves and our incinerated ashes wandering, racing about, purging our impatient interminable wasteland.

Our recollections of a fresh light and our primal scream at birth, sounded as the echo of a trumpet signaling bliss in a naked dream. It offered us a ride on a freight car to the credo of earthly immortality.

Surveying the vision, my primal sight soon came to the realization that these tender joys would last, with the proviso that our ghostly memory allowed before relinquishing to the tide of time and light fluttering as a promise.

Sprinkled dust came in the robe that promptly covered me, dissipating the cast of shadows which challenged my evident tears for sorrows. From then on continued silence beyond broken promises elude us all.

The only oath we can all count on are those held deep in our own heart and soul.

July 01, 1989

AT THE OUTSET OF A JOURNEY

As I pass the wooden corridors filled with ghostly stillness, a shapeless mass of burning... fading, plagued silence awaits me.

A long and thick forest of soundless notes accost me for what seems to be long hours of purgatory before I awaken to wonders.

I endlessly walk streets that already have my name, as I weave light post after light post, mapping a nimble journey at the edge of avid gardens.

Sullen winds wander, circling past the ashen landscape filled with air currents that bring immolated dreams as compost for a whispering Earth.

I navigate on rails ignited by the brush fires in the night sky, breathing distances created from the outset of our primal mutterings.

Miles and miles away from completing my destiny, a stirring dusk is piercing the roots of my brawling fathomless future in collision with the Earth.

Invisible ghosts are still approaching my imminent unfolding / barricaded bay where I am swashbuckling my own roaring shadow.

September 16, 2013

ODE TO THE DARK SHADOWS

I sing to the dark shadows for those rescued from murky rivers of
gloom, the same that strolled through forests of night to speak
with the dead over meadows of silence and proud
seeds of nothingness.

I sing equally to the secret lakes filled from puddles of mournful dark
waters that stroll over fields of granite, naked Irises,
Lilies and Hydrangeas.

I intone notes that accompany the lost dawns of steel, whose advent
of daybreak enlightens and spreads as petals and ballads travel
on the back of stray groaning winds.

As the Goldfinch's song scatters dawns of primitive hope and brio,
I sing to the rain to counter dark purple auroras and veils of stone.

I want to sing to the brunette shadows that sow comfort on homes of
rubble, seedbeds of subdued extinguished seas, caves of bodies in
violent silence wailing forever resting on tombs deprived of
any calming wind and consoling music.

I rest on tombs deprived of threatening winds and mysterious consoling music.

I sing an Ode to the dark shadows!

July 11, 2011 – July 14, 2015

AQUARELLE

My palm solemnly dips into the aquarelle which depicts
my face covered in winter dust and wearing
a crown made of icicles.

It thaws before your gaze. It smiles as it dresses in the
harbors of your heart and unpacks the invasive raw
quiet desolation of the cold.

I am only protected from the upcoming winter storm
By the canvas' borders which ride on
cirrus fermented rails.

June 02, 1985

DISEMBARKING

Living as a bystander clasping onto a swift assemblage
of fountains, winking with scorn at handmade muted
moons, I am smiling and grinning even through my
teeth are plagued with neglect.

We are disembarking on top of quiet illusions incubated
by the winds of Spring, Summer and Autumn, not
Winter, just episodic declarative
conclusions for now.

We believe in detours away from the obedient footprint
that leashes onto mystic shores and its montage
of images that buries this footage in the deep
recesses of our pre- frontal lobe.

The evidence of wounded dazed witnesses lurching
for hope is a recurrent memory that transits
among the synapses in our universe.

Let's go ashore to hear clandestine planets to ruminate and hope!

February 21, 2018

THE WORDS IN MY POEMS

*My words dress in autumn leaves to disguise that Winter has
arrived. Time is ploddingly waning.*

*Amid seldom seen nights, the words grow somber and are barely
audible, as the voice of an ancient owl in an old barn.
The words crawl out in between the venerable wooden planks.*

*Utterances now sleep at the shores of mythic history and are
towed by their punctuation marks that are used
as walking sticks.*

*The lines of the letters are losing their sharpened edges and are
getting scraggly and broken. But its epistolary meaning
still has its resonance.*

*My poignant expressions have been windswept toward the
unknown shores of a song that growls and moans
its history.*

*Sometimes words are coming as celestial written mist that exist
un-fissured in a liquid rusted reality that gets its inspiration
from the shadow of its origin.*

December 12, 1994

DISTANT CREATION

*Wistfully the birch trees speak as the voice of the forest. they
visit the early morning exhorting the mountain's scars
clawing out of the shadows to be born.*

*You are a distant creation with a non-compliant soul, you unfold
your breast to the earth, your body to Apollo, your spirit to
the gods, your heart to Aphrodite and your half-eaten food
to the rest of us!*

*The nests on top of pine trees brighten the unfolding day as it
travels hoisting spring mornings before they spatter
themselves as a Jackson Pollock creation over
the world's canvas.*

*Imagined peace and harmony are just a distant creation
embedded and unbroken in the sky's thunder mastering
the flowering sorrows protesting our tranquility.*

*Silence always arrives at midnight after its partial journey
riding on muted spotted sounds emanating from the
heart's sun in conflict after its genesis.*

*Gushing winds are pushing the air currents behind the
bird's flight drinking the space deciphering the
inquisitive praise of angels complementing
our flying skills.*

August 01, 2017

REAWAKENING

Landscapes of rose bushes roll-by my heart's window pulsing midnight dream truths melting into the core of unremembered darkness, as I say words that break silence and stain pages under mass-produced moonlight.

I'm emerging chirping away from the kleptomaniacal journey that takes away from the healing storm as well as nests rousing hands waiting for me, stirring, as I lash-on to Spring's shadow.

Immutable confessions from my heart are telling me that pausing to be embraced by you, is like the moss, tree and flowers waiting to drink-in the rain. They are pantomiming chains of black and white symbols waiting to [blossom]giving birth.

Your moon seduces and nourishes me, as I traverse your sacred mounds, where I shudder along with my living dreams accompanying hybrid wounds bruised under your howling, but harmless light.

I want to be held within the grasp and distance of your body and soul, ahead of lost earthworms blinking before they whittle themselves into carcasses of re-awakened compost yearning... at the intersection of life and death.

Re-awaken my sparks before they reach gleaming extinction, as I populate veined torments...slaughtered while I'm immersed in your eyes' glance hurtling clawing unto promise's wagon wheels.

April 01, 2007

VOICELESS HABITATS

The shade gathers on your ramshackle lands before the
foretold storms of autumn advance on your grieving
sodden earth vowing to the discharging bursting
storm rising before your undefined winter.

Empty roadhouses on fire are crowding the voices
of our mate less souls in a battle to take back
from the tempest the marrow of our destiny
living in voiceless abodes.

The riots in our land are disrupting our peach-blossomed
songs, before derailing them completely by the
parallel inferno accosting our flesh.

Millennial questions abound before being admonished
by the non-existent gods expanding our latched
sorrows.

We still live in voiceless habitats of awakened lamentations
beyond borders. Without witnessing the flickering
lights at the dock which seizes the touch of the
meditative cosmos that is sweeping the
atoms and particles of our being.

August 22, 2003 – August 22, 2016

TWILIGHT

*The tired twilight seeks refuge and snuggles in with the shadows
of marble that converses with vanishing moons before they
forget our reciprocal language.*

*In exiled corners, old memories speak with women and the fireflies
that light up the exalted life that is sitting on blue marble.*

*The wind narrates a story that strikes forlorn hearts while they
are marching enigmatically in the direction of our past
which sleeps on the restless sea foam.*

*I disguise myself as a tree in a forest just to pretend that
I am indeed alone.*

*The Sun bleeds and my body rests on the districts of cold blue
marble, lit by the light of a well-worn twilight.*

November 11, 2014 - October 07, 2015

AMID EXPLORING NIGHTS

*I wince and weep as bundles of recently reaped dreams roll on
the deserted fields of my brain. They dismantle themselves in
the midst of rudderless time as scrap metal in the urban
junkyard of my existence.*

*Wraiths escape my unpredictable night ballads harvested under
rivers of thoughts and invented sounds found within the
confines of my temples, a mixing bowl of broken screams
and limbs of voiced nightmares are following me*

*Amid exploring night visions, sheaves of specters emanate from their
sockets, divorcing themselves from their moorings, rolling toward
bewildering streams, where a multitude of cuffed mortals
drowned in rapids of twilight waters.*

*It is the law of un-punctuated lost sentences and random lives that
withdraw themselves from LIFE as vanished saints and untold
unpredictable gods who have gone before them.*

*Amid exploring nights, unwritten invented births dissipate in Freudian
and Jungian forged moon river's wombs.*

March 28, 2015

MISTRESS OF OUR WINDOW

To mom:

*On the other side of the pane, the rain strolls to dampen the sun
rays as well as the feathers of a flock of your beloved
"NY pigeons".*

*Inside your chest cavity, your heart is dampened too, as I think
you are imagining the fertile land from whence you
came. You are alone.*

*Your eyes are watered from the rain as well, as you have
opened the window. The soul of the night is showing
its shadow and its scent is stewing in the dark*

*It reminds me of the metal petals being pounded on an anvil,
just to be strung on a clothesline in new-born alleys,
confessor the streets, rain and fields is to the
window pane in the midst of an intense interlude*

*Messengers are blithely raking in fish engulfed in nestling
naked mud built in the river.*

*You observe the heart of the city through a silent dream
walking hand in hand with grieving, smiling eternal hope,
flaunting while touching the skin of the night of our
neighbors*

August 22, 1989

THE DEATH OF A POEM

*Its death came about after imitating one of its lines. Its words
and its soul shattered amid a barrage of images fusing
the ontological with a cubist reality.*

*Its strophes amalgamated with preludes of colors and aromas
with the essence of dusk and its hues of withering fire,
its stanzas with rage thrown toward sea hills ablaze.*

*The moist terrain where youth awaits us in is dimly lit by the snow
light kneeling above the gardens of mid-summer where I live
unchained to particles only weighted by the lead of my pen.*

*At last, let's set floodlights on tombs for collapsible time, seduce
all flowers that nap on barbed-wire and unabashedly rest
on the edge of sunlight with wings.*

*I ride on parallel lines, hauling stars to trap them until they
dock in my heart!*

*Cataclysmic dispersal of layers of salient words gather clandestine
pixels so you can recognize me in your memory.*

*The night train time collapses into naked translations which travel
In the direction of homeless riverbeds under a vanishing solstice.*

*I'll cover you with a collapsible alphabet collage to wear my words
as a robe of defrosted whispers. thunder and rain.*

*Please expatriate my skin and my bones to layered subdued
horizons of a silent vermillion*

MAY 07, 2015

OUR TUMULTUOUS STORY

Behind our narrative, we are being reduced to false aged dispatches that exist only in the expansive shores of a borrowed imagination.

We are emerging from storms that washed away the sand from our clock...the oxygen from our air and the light from our shadow.

We are running away holding hands with the fog.

November 28, 2013

I TRAVELLED NORTH

I travelled northward on sailing winds pulling me away from the
Andes mountains, where my bones were birthed in a mist under
the stars of the South Sea's apprehended imprint and escaping
parade of wandering drifting stars.

I did not make the choice. It was made for me by my destiny
and the trumpeting gods that forgot that there was and still
is life past the relevant frowned upon 23rd parallel.

Journeying to the kingdom of the North rocked the south of my
soul, even when I crossed past the Tropic of Cancer, past the
draught and unfaithful spirits not speaking my
centrifugal fluttering story.

I'll narrate my story. It was that of a hungry child looking for dreams
to entering through forbidden vanishing doors as I voyaged toward
the northern latitudes, leaving my friends and family seeking
the miracle of life alongside my Mother.

I was not greeted by birds, but with songs infused with collateral
relentless car noises drowning the rich silence billowing up from
the intrusive white concrete. Somehow, I persevered
as all émigrés do.

In the aftermath of unfurling my path toward the broadening horizons,
I am now imbedded with souls who still taunt and bully my space
in an ever interminable pregnant ripple.

I am a disciple of conjured dreams outside the boundaries and
exploratory forays in an existential quest seeking a new meaning
to life in new free lands under the crepuscule of stars.

Still, I feel as though I have been vanished from my land and living
in conflicted singed borrowed shadows seared forever in
my misplaced heart.

May 01, 1990 – May 01, 2015

47

LOVING RAIN

I drink the interim sweet beauty of your gentle rain. I bathe in this loving purifying silent waters before it rambles in search of an apocryphal direction.

This rain falls asleep and hides from the shipwreck that is the genesis of my dream, encountering an upended boat, slipping and sliding in blooming waves flooding my unframed face.

Showers came as an unfulfilled promise washing away and robbing the script from mother nature, taking down the flooded road slammed with water defying acumen and hope.

Deluge earnestly filled the afternoon with waters and lingering puddles that ambled over landscapes well marked by indelible water marks as evidence of footsteps in the rain.

Let me ponder this megalithic silken dream which defoliates and washes my humanity and essence. I think it was wreathed out of ashes and rainwater behind the cosmic windowsill.

Oct. 25, 1991 – Feb 03, 2014

THE CONFESSIONS OF SCARS

The range of voices emanating from our walls are
breaking through silence. they are walking on
riverbeds that whisper their scabs; replicas
of messages from the life, water and mud
that hums and huddles in unison as
they rest on our flesh.

Painted blisters from our eyelids all the way to our
bone marrow are racing past the raging fire that
is consuming my cell's shelter.

The spring waters of midnight are washing
the cicatrices in and out of my body as we
are being adopted by the neglected lights
belonging to some forgotten heretical
shadows feeding the night's hunger.

Under silent dawns, wounds are mounted
on our body as sleeves twirling the
air on flung fluted currents close
to the mystical gates where we
leave proof of our existence.

Slain dragons are in the sky's attic
clenching and chomping on our flesh
and bones, as our hushed cries speak
of our atomic existence hiding
behind the anguished blemishes of
my darkened soil.

We are saddling to ride on fierce rivers
breathing fire, ice and the fading light
on the horizon overwhelming the
chrysanthemum and lilac flowers
scarring our purview.

September 27, 2017

LOOKING FOR WATER TRAILS

When I was a young boy, wherever I went, I'd see you inside my eyes
caressing the roses that live in my heart mischievously and
magically crossing over a world converging within the
veins of my heart.

They were transporting the echoes of my mission one started
once started in the reverberation of my lonely dreams.

Water Lilies were prancing on rainwater splashing, not trying to
lose their equilibrium in the pads where us and other species
were drowning our sorrows wafting in lily ponds.

In the tree of life, you represent beauty, fragrance and the
ultimate explanation of ethereal evolution, rebirth and
the return to safe waterways after copious rains.

Water trails are mapped in mine and your brain as a symbol
of discovery, adventure and the endless paddling we must
make on our journey, while we cross the endless trails
in search of lost hearts to love and heal.

Under bright lights gleaming in flux to darkness, I find myself as
a ship's captain dithering between currents, suffering in deep
waters attempting to persuade the streams to allow me
to prevail onto my destination hidden behind water
gardens of spiritual enlighten.

Water lilies and I are both clades in the breast of
this aquatic planet!

February 21, 1969

NO MORE RIVERS OF SORROW

No more sorrow. I can't lose you, I am coming back to
drink from your waterfall's alluring water as it
gently caresses even its most lacerated rocks.

As your river meanders my heart sings again like the warbler
on a cold pine forest branch in a Michigan winter and a
Nashville warbler's two-note phrase without its trill.

I've suffered misery while riding rising waters on your river
that forced me into a runnel that defines the borders
between the sorrows and us.

Its braided waters spill over my heart where it steers flowing
over its riverbeds washing our body with mud. Please no
more. No more rivers of sorrow.

River of sorrow i can still retrace your rogue silent cartilage
bends with my finger. I can still taste your lush ice-cold
water and its sweetness with my lips.

September 07, 2016

I AM STUMBLING AND LIMPING ABOUT

*My future seems uncertain. I have no fixed destination. I am docked in the fog
I am wandering towards a prearranged destiny*

*I think I'll hide in the unfathomable and impenetrable memory of the look
in your eyes as it was strolling on the sidewalks of my heart.*

Perhaps I should melt and merge along with the black orchids...

*The dew of the heavens is caressing my ephemeral tears, as they stumble down
the cliffs of my cheekbones. I am wandering towards a prearranged destiny.*

*I heard the forgotten psalms in the garden where ardor and silence repose.
They reminded me of the urgency with which life's loving glance
communicates the beauty of love.*

*I recall that it was resting on a branch of the of life which then subtly took
refuge in the last shadow before migrating towards oblivion.*

*The earth is always the messenger and chronicler of loves and life that are
briefly united as they parade in a common promenade.
Some give love to unworthy characters, while other heartless ones, never
give anything but venom and concealed resentment.*

*I don't want the shadows to overwhelm my empty solitude and embrace
me like an Anaconda. Though I am stumbling about and limping,
I'm breathing freely and know that I'm not under bondage.*

*Let silence sing a song of hope, while we wander towards a prearranged
destiny. won't you come along!*

March 07, 2001 – March 11, 2016